Animals on the Job

By Nancy E. Krulik

SCHOLASTIC INC.

New York   Toronto   London   Auckland   Sydney

For Danny

Photos: COVER: *St. Bernard*: © Bruce Coleman, Inc.; *Elephant*: © Mickey Gibson/Animals, Animals; *Sled Dogs*: © Agence Vandystadt, Paris, France/Photo Researchers, Inc.; *Bottle-Nosed Dolphin*: © Nicholas Conte/Bruce Coleman, Inc. INTERIOR: *Huskies*: © Agence Vandystadt, Paris, France/Photo Researchers, Inc.; *St. Bernard*: © 1978 Frank Roche/Animals, Animals; *Seeing Eye Dog*: © 1988 Lawrence Migdale/Photo Researchers, Inc.; *Herd Dog*: © J. Burt/Bruce Coleman, Inc.; *Benji*: © Mulberry Square Productions, Inc.; *Police Horses*: © 1989 Andrew Dalsimer/Bruce Coleman, Inc.; *Cowboy and Horse*: © 1983 Rosalie LaRue Faubion/Bruce Coleman, Inc.; *Cat*: © 1987 Hans Reinhard/Bruce Coleman, Inc.; *Capuchin Monkey*: © 1988 Jose Azel/Contact Press Images; *Homing Pigeons*: © Tom McHugh/Photo Researchers Inc.; *Camel*: © Mickey Gibson/Animals, Animals; *Elephants*: © Brian Carroll/Bruce Coleman, Inc.; *Llama* © 1988 Bruce Coleman, Inc.; *Tigers*: © 1983 Bill Bachman/Photo Researchers, Inc.; *Dolphin*: © Wardene Weisser/Bruce Coleman, Inc.; *Parakeet*: © John Kaprielian/Photo Researchers, Inc.; *Parakeet*: © Robert Pearcy/Animals, Animals; *Guinea Pig*: © Richard Kolar Animals, Animals; *Hamster*: © Hans Reinhard/Bruce Coleman, Inc.

Special thanks to Deborah Thompson for her photo research.

ISBN 0-590-42986-8

12 11 10 9 8 7 6 5 4 3   2 3 4 5/9

Printed in the U.S.A.   23
First Scholastic printing, February 1990.

What kinds of jobs do animals have?

They help the police catch criminals.
They help handicapped people cross the street.
They carry wood for construction workers.
They even star in movies!

Many animals can be taught to work with people.
Let's meet some animals that have jobs.

Huskies pull sleds
in places where it is very cold.
They carry Eskimo people and supplies
from place to place.
The dog in the front
listens to the sled driver.
He must learn Eskimo words like *huk*,
which means go on;
howeh, which means turn right;
and *ashoo*,
which means go left.

Sometimes, when there has been an earthquake,
people get trapped under fallen buildings.
Rescue workers can not see them,
but rescue dogs can use their strong
sense of smell
to find the trapped people
and save their lives.
Newfoundland dogs make good rescue dogs.

St. Bernards rescue people
who get lost during snowstorms
and might be buried under the snow.
It's a *ruff* job,
but the St. Bernards work hard to save lives!

Seeing Eye dogs
help people who can not see.
Seeing Eye dogs go to school
to learn how to lead blind people
safely across the street.
They learn to help blind people walk
without bumping into things.
Most animals are not allowed
in restaurants or on buses and trains.
But Seeing Eye dogs can go
wherever their owners go.

On the farm,
herd dogs take care
of the sheep.
During the day they make sure
no sheep wanders off
and gets lost.
At night they guard the sheep
against wild animals
who might want to eat them.

Benji has a great job
as an actor in the movies.
Benji travels first class on airplanes,
stays in fancy hotels, and eats steak for dinner,
just like any other movie star.
But Benji and his trainer, Frank Inn, also work very hard,
making sure Benji learns all of his tricks.

Horses can have many jobs.
Some horses help police officers catch criminals.
A police officer can see better
when he or she sits high up on a horse's back.
Horses can walk down paths
that are too narrow for cars.

Farm horses help farmers pull plows and wagons
across land that is too steep or muddy
for tractors to drive through.

The cowboy's horse must be very fast
to help him herd cattle. Giddyap!

The farm cat works very hard.
She can not spend the whole day
curled up in a soft easy chair,
like a pet cat in the city can.
The farm cat keeps busy
catching mice.
When the farm cat catches a mouse,
the farmer gives her a big saucer of milk
as a reward.

The people who live with capuchin monkeys know
that monkey business is serious business!
Capuchin monkeys live with people
who can not move their arms and legs.
They are trained to do simple tasks
that will help their masters
live more normal lives.
Capuchin monkeys can pick up things that
have fallen on the floor.
They can get sandwiches or drinks
from the refrigerator.
They can even put movie cassettes
into a VCR!

Homing pigeons are feathered mail carriers.
They are trained to carry messages
from strange places back to their homes.
The note is placed in a special container
on the pigeon's back.
Homing pigeons deliver their messages very quickly.
They can fly as fast as 60 miles an hour.
That's faster than a car goes on the highway!

Some people call camels the ships of the desert.
That's because camels carry people and supplies
across the hot desert sand,
just like boats carry people and supplies over water.

In the desert, water and food are hard to find.
Luckily, a camel can travel for a long time without getting thirsty.
The hump on the camel's back is made of fat.
While he waits for food,
the camel can live off the fat in its hump for many days.

Indian elephants work in lumber camps in Asia.
The elephants are very strong.
They can lift a ton of logs with their trunks!

Sometimes the elephants work in pairs.
They stand shoulder to shoulder.
Then, together, they roll the heavy logs
into piles.
Heave ho!

Llamas are very important
to the people who live
way up in the Andes Mountains
of South America.
The people need the llamas
to carry heavy bags up the steep mountain paths.
Llamas have sharp hoofs
to help them climb.

Tigers in the circus work all year long.
Animal trainers teach them tricks.
The tigers learn to jump through fiery hoops
and sit up on their hind legs.
Circus tigers always make the audience
roar with delight!

Some dolphins work in water shows.
They jump high in the air
and eat from a person's hand.
They play catch with big plastic balls.
They can even shake hands with their flippers.
When the crowd cheers, the dolphins take a bow.
Hooray!

Pets have special jobs, too.
They make you feel happy when you are sad.
They make you laugh.
When you have a pet,
you are never lonely.
A pet's job is to be your friend.
That's one job that isn't hard at all.